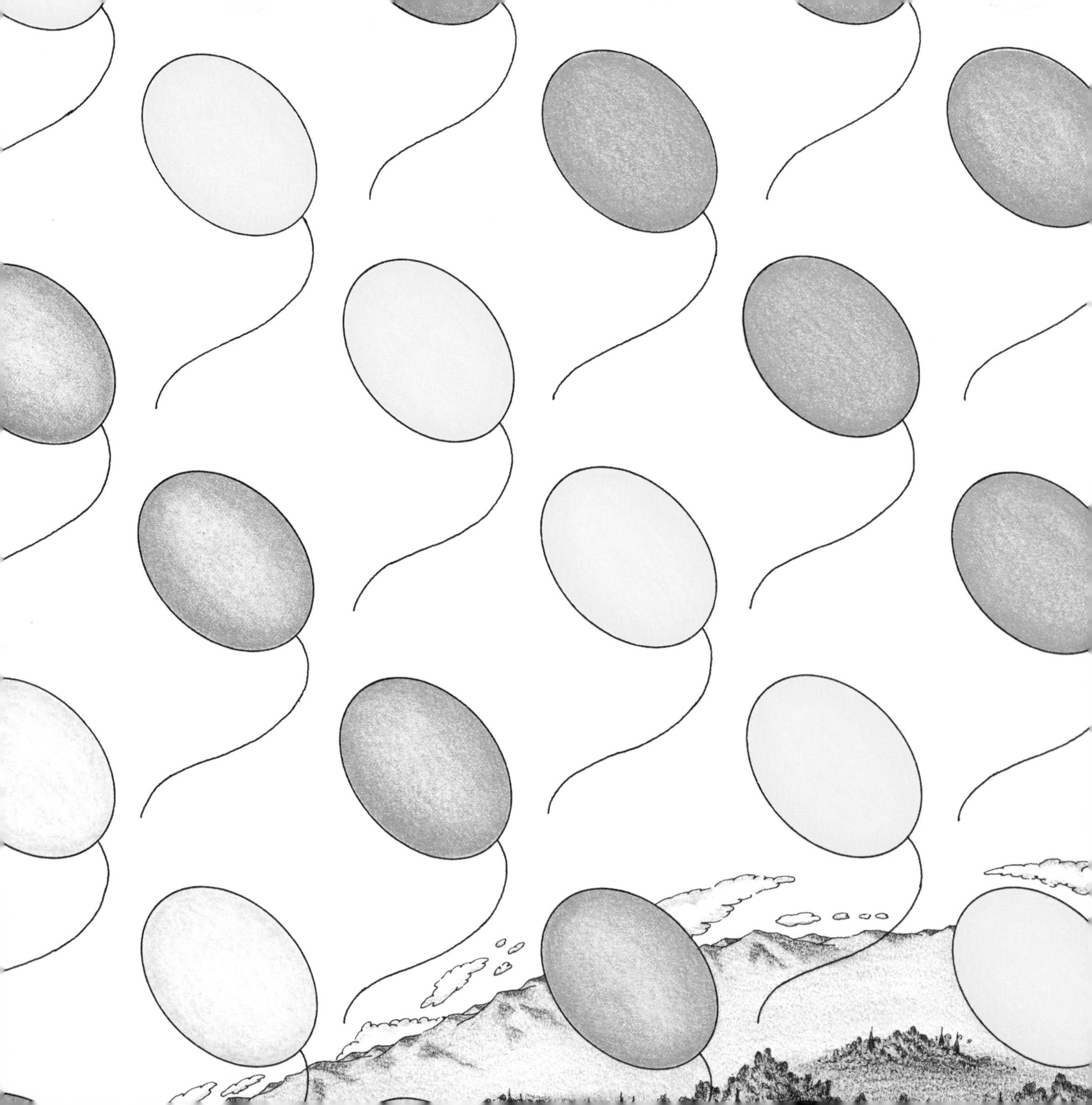

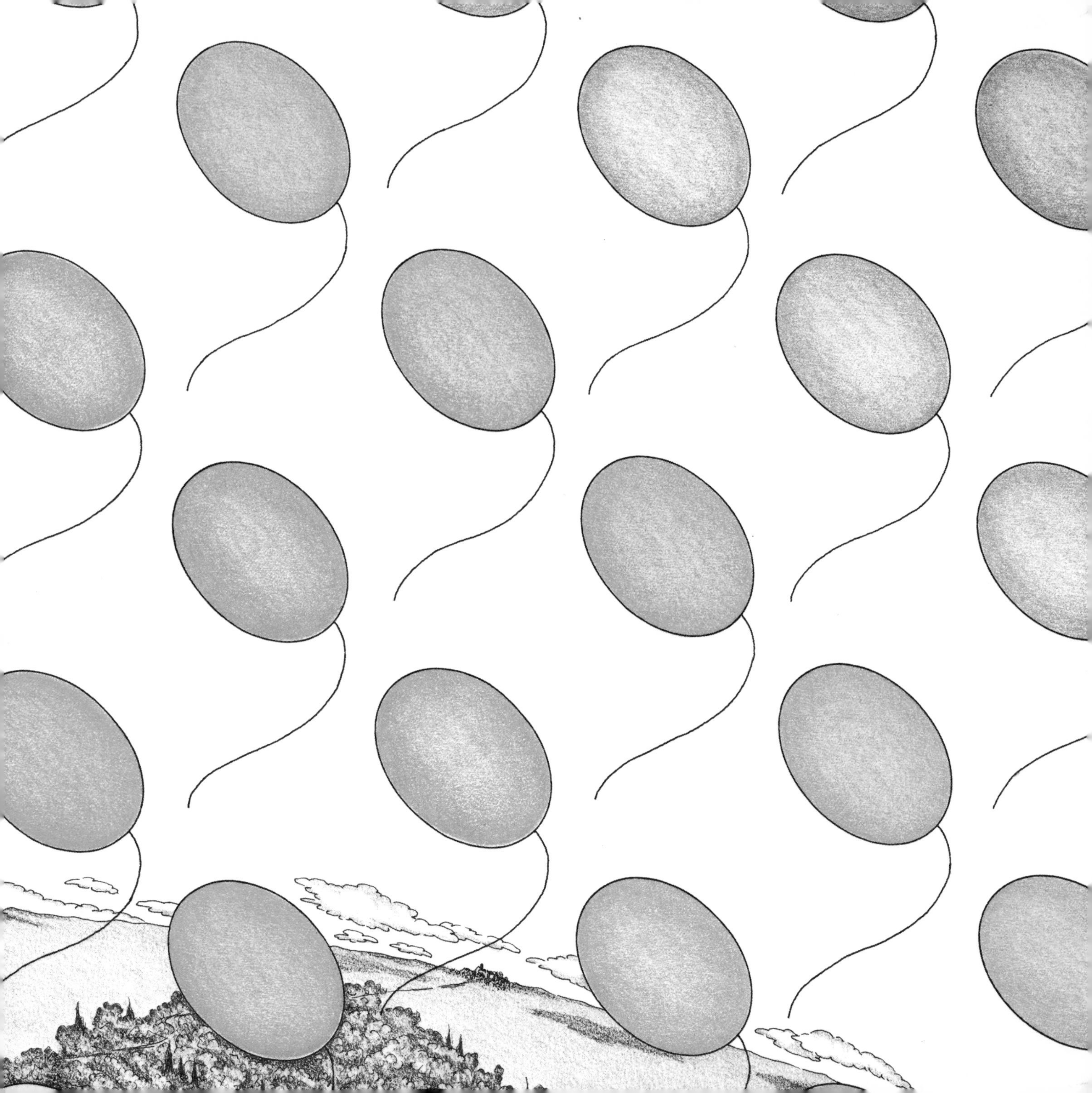

For Michael and Jolie

Clarion Books
a Houghton Mifflin Company imprint
215 Park Avenue South, New York, NY 10003

Printed in the USA

Library of Congress Cataloging in Publication Data
Peek, Merle.
Mary wore her red dress, and Henry wore his
green sneakers.
Summary: Each of Katy Bear's animal friends wears a
different color of clothing to her birthday party.
1. Children's stories, American. [1. Color—
Fiction. 2. Animals—Fiction. 3. Parties—Fiction]
I. Title.
PZ7.P346Mar 1985 [E] 84-12733
ISBN 0-89919-324-2 PA ISBN 0-89919-701-9

WOZ 30 29 28

MARY WORE HER RED DRESS,
RED DRESS, RED DRESS,

MARY WORE HER RED DRESS
ALL DAY LONG.

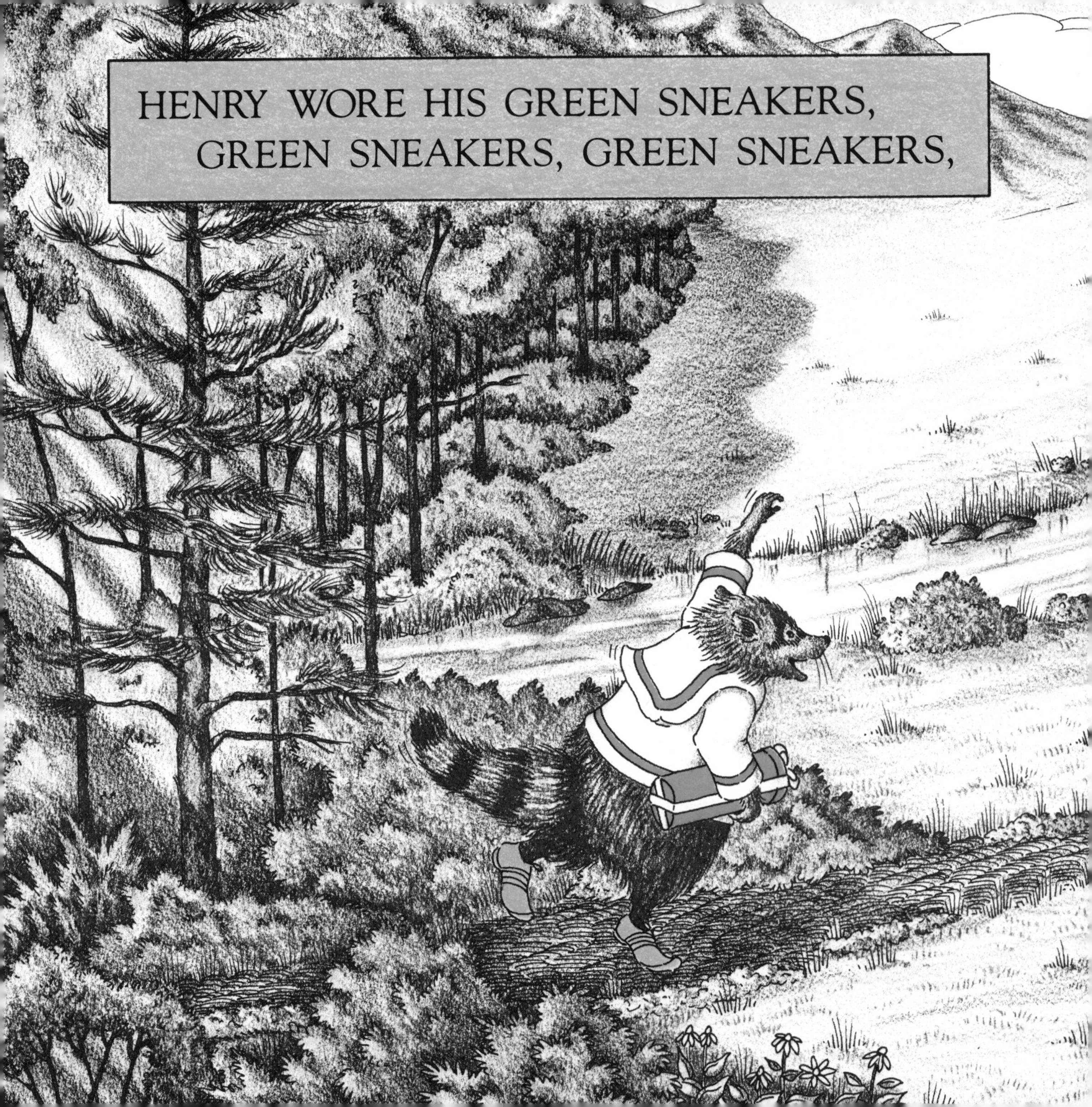
HENRY WORE HIS GREEN SNEAKERS,
GREEN SNEAKERS, GREEN SNEAKERS,

HENRY WORE HIS GREEN SNEAKERS
ALL DAY LONG.

KATY WORE HER YELLOW SWEATER,
YELLOW SWEATER, YELLOW SWEATER,

KATY WORE HER YELLOW SWEATER
ALL DAY LONG.

BEN WORE HIS BLUE JEANS,
BLUE JEANS, BLUE JEANS,

BEN WORE HIS BLUE JEANS
ALL DAY LONG.

AMANDA WORE HER BROWN BANDANA,
BROWN BANDANA, BROWN BANDANA,

AMANDA WORE HER BROWN BANDANA
ALL DAY LONG.

RYAN WORE HIS PURPLE PANTS,
PURPLE PANTS, PURPLE PANTS,

RYAN WORE HIS PURPLE PANTS
ALL DAY LONG.

STACY WORE HER VIOLET RIBBONS,
VIOLET RIBBONS, VIOLET RIBBONS,

STACY WORE HER VIOLET RIBBONS
ALL DAY LONG.

KENNY WORE HIS ORANGE SHIRT,
ORANGE SHIRT, ORANGE SHIRT,

KENNY WORE HIS ORANGE SHIRT
ALL DAY LONG.

WHO WORE A PINK HAT,
PINK HAT, PINK HAT,

WHO WORE A PINK HAT
ALL DAY LONG?

KATY WORE A PINK HAT,
PINK HAT, PINK HAT,

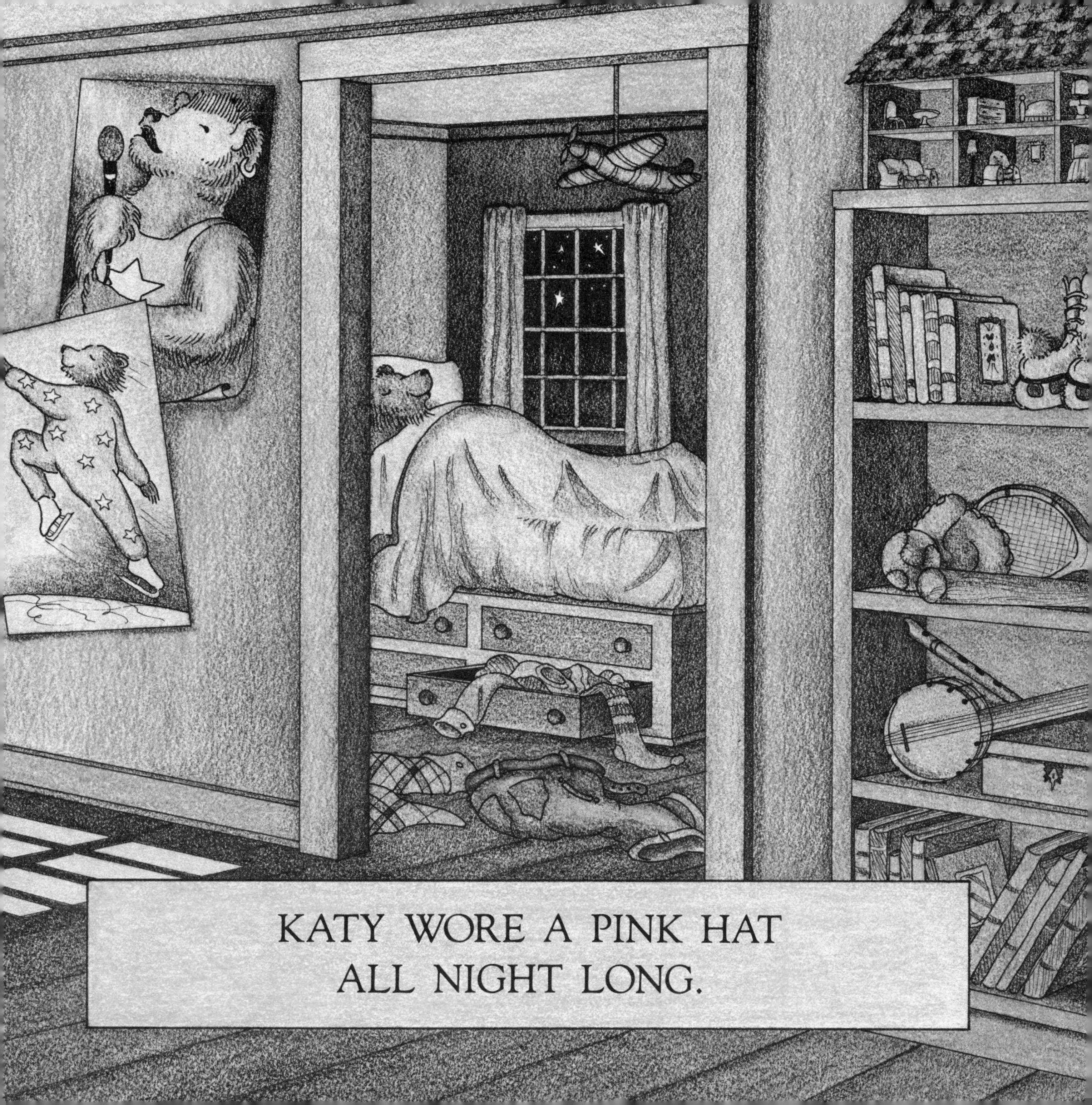
KATY WORE A PINK HAT
ALL NIGHT LONG.

Mary Wore Her Red Dress . . . .

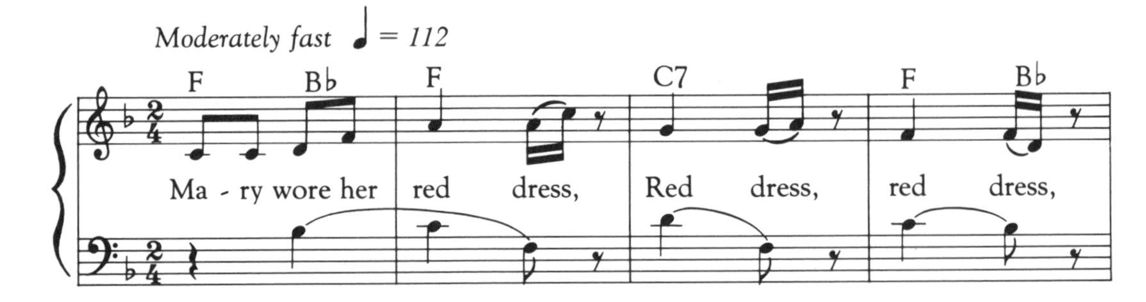

2. Henry wore his green sneakers,
   Green sneakers, green sneakers,
   Henry wore his green sneakers
   All day long.
3. Katy wore her yellow sweater, etc.
4. Ben wore his blue jeans, etc.
5. Amanda wore her brown bandana, etc.
6. Ryan wore his purple pants, etc.
7. Stacy wore her violet ribbons, etc.
8. Kenny wore his orange shirt, etc.
9. Who wore a pink hat, etc.
10. Katy wore a pink hat, etc.

A Note from the Author

Mary Wore Her Red Dress is a folk song from Texas, and it lends itself well to improvisation. Children can make up verses about themselves and their friends. It doesn't matter if the new items are too long to fit the music; just add the necessary number of beats to fit the syllables as in *Julie wore her green-and-blue-striped overalls, her green-and-blue striped overalls . . . .*

Besides singing about clothing and colors, the possibilities for other verses are endless. Daily incidents can inspire them—outside it's raining; the tulips are blooming; the dog is sleeping. Along those lines, the children could sing *Barry is running in the rain, in the rain . . .; David picked some red tulips, red tulips . . .; Daisy took a nap by the fire, a nap by the fire. . . .*

A guessing game is always fun. The children might begin with *Who's got a bandaged finger, bandaged finger . . .? Sydney has a bandaged finger, bandaged finger. . . .* Then they could go on with *Who has a new kitty, new kitty . . .? Alice has a new kitty, new kitty, new kitty, Alice has a new kitty, all day long.*

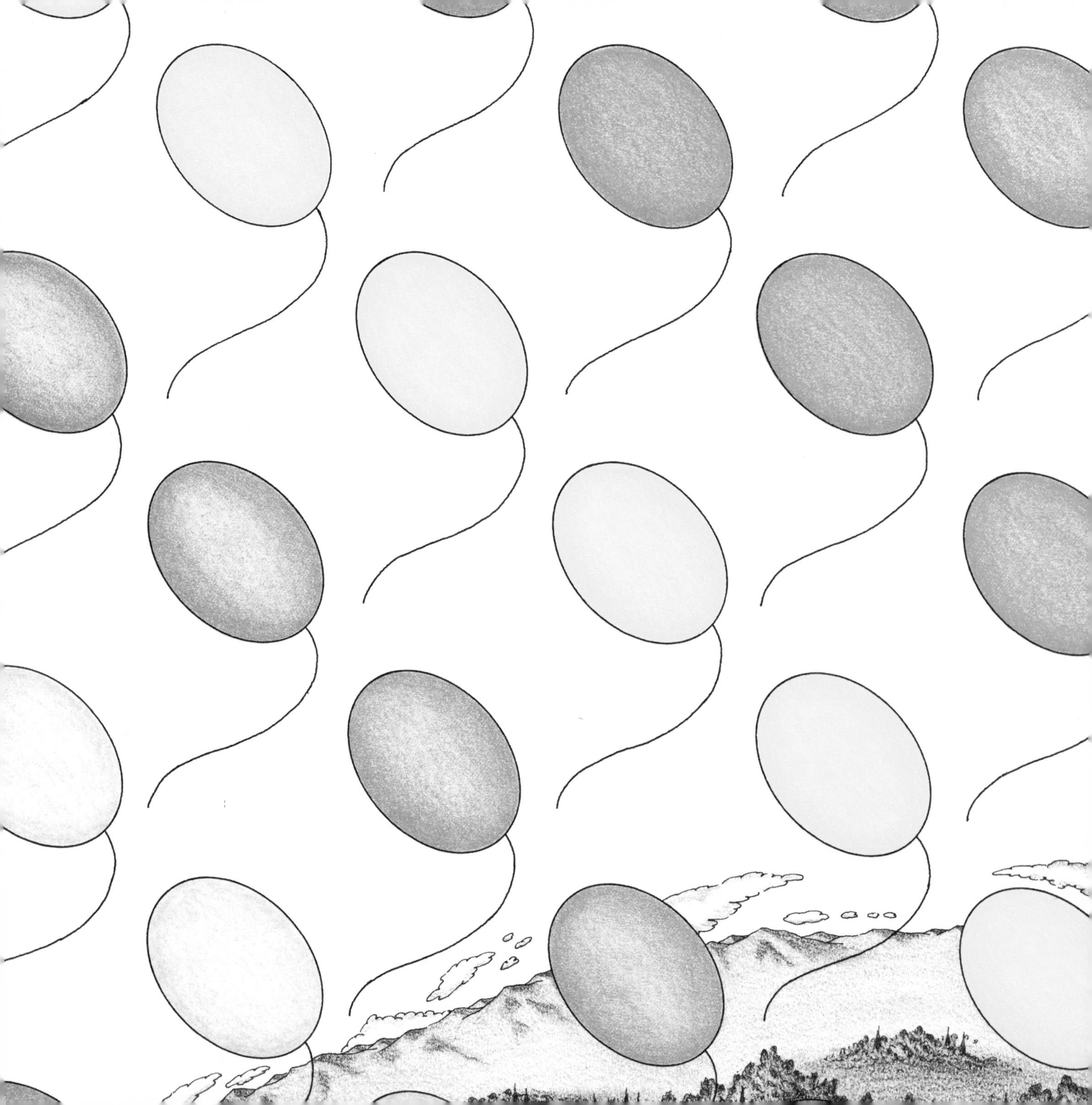

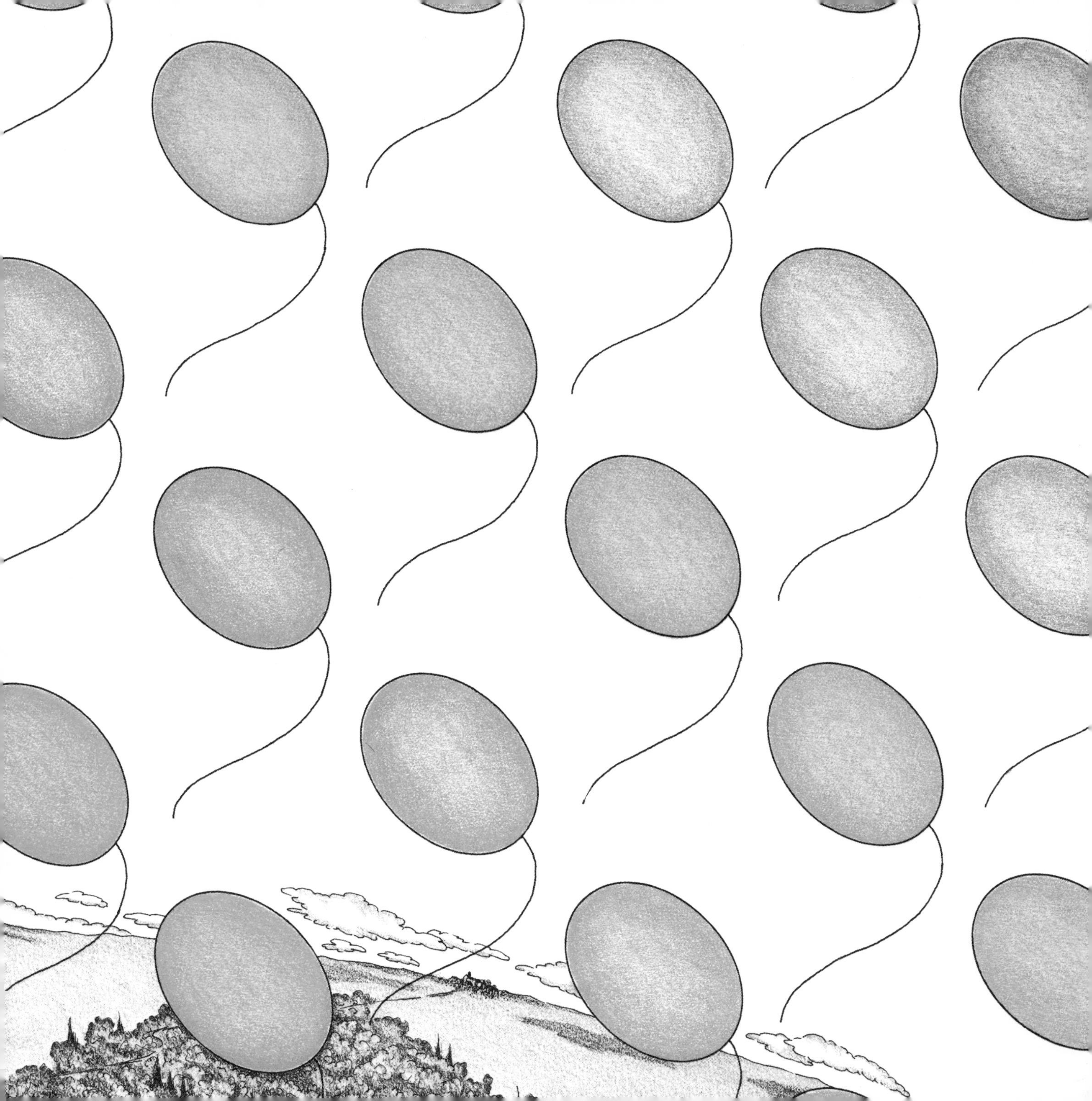

HCOLX +
E
PEEK